The Storm

For my wife, Lucy Curtin, who helped draft these stories
inspired by the animals of her own childhood.

First published in 2009
by Wayland

This paperback edition published in 2010 by Wayland

Text copyright © Peter Bently 2009
Illustration copyright © Elisabetta Ferrero 2009

Wayland
338 Euston Road
London NW1 3BH

Wayland Australia
Level 17/207 Kent Street
Sydney, NSW 2000

The rights of Peter Bently to be identified as the Author
and Elisabetta Ferrero to be identified as the Illustrator of this Work have
been asserted by them in accordance with the Copyright, Designs and
Patents Act, 1988.

Series Editor: Louise John
Editor: Katie Powell
Cover design: Paul Cherrill
Design: D.R.ink
Consultant: Shirley Bickler

A CIP catalogue record for this book is available from the British Library.

ISBN 9780750256803 (hbk)
ISBN 9780750259910 (pbk)

The Storm

Written by Peter Bently
Illustrated by Elisabetta Ferrero

WAYLAND

Tara lived at Starcross Stables with her mum, her dad and a sheepdog called Rocket.

They had a shire horse called Plod, a little pony called Rascal, and a donkey called Smokey.

One day, Rascal, Smokey and Plod were in the field with Dad, who was mending his tractor.

"Come on, Rocket," said Tara. "Let's go and help him!"

Just then, there was a rumble
in the sky.

"I hear thunder!" said Tara.

"There's going to be a storm,"
said Mum.

The sky went dark and it started to rain.

"Quick!" shouted Dad. "Run to the stable. It's closer than the house!"

"Look at the animals!" cried Tara.
Rascal, Smokey and Plod were
running up the field.

"They'll be OK. They're going
to shelter under the big tree,"
said Dad.

Rascal and Smokey ran on ahead.
Plod trotted behind them.

"Hurry up, Plod!" called Tara.
"Catch up!"

11

Rascal and Smokey reached the
tree first.

"Plod's a silly old slowcoach!"
laughed Tara.

There was a flash of lightning and a clap of thunder. The storm was getting worse.

Rocket was scared and hid in the straw.

Then, Tara and Dad heard
a loud CRACK!

"Look!" cried Tara. "The big tree
has been struck by lightning!"

The tree fell to the ground with a thud, trapping Rascal and Smokey.

"Come on!" said Dad. "We need to free them!"

Tara and Dad ran back to the field.
Rocket followed behind.

"He wants to help," said Tara.
"Brave boy, Rocket!"

"I'm not sure how we're going to move the tree," said Dad. "We'll need to be quick. Rascal and Smokey are getting scared."

"Could we use the tractor?"
asked Tara.

"No," said Dad, shaking his head.
"I didn't finish mending it."

"Daisy's dad has a tractor too!"
said Tara. Daisy was Tara's
best friend.

"But they're on holiday," said Dad.

Plod neighed to Rascal and Smokey.
"I know," said Tara. "Plod can
help us!"

Dad brought Plod's harness from the stable, and Tara carried some strong ropes.

Tara helped Dad to put on Plod's heavy harness.

Then, Tara tied one end of the rope to the harness. Dad fastened the other end around the tree.

Plod started to pull, but the tree didn't move.

"It's too heavy!" said Dad.

"Come on, Plod," said Tara, kindly. "You can do it, boy!"

Plod heaved with all his might.
Slowly the tree started to move.

"Hooray!" cried Tara. "That's it!
Keep pulling, Plod!"

At last, Rascal and Smokey were free. They galloped happily around the field.

Rocket gave a loud, "Woof!" and ran after them.

"Well done, Plod!" said Tara.
"I'm really sorry I laughed at you.
You're only slow because you're so
big and strong."

"I think Plod needs a big bucket of carrots!" said Dad.

"Yes," said Mum, coming into the field. "And we all need some dry clothes!"

START READING is a series of highly enjoyable books for beginner readers. **The books have been carefully graded to match the Book Bands widely used in schools.** This enables readers to be sure they choose books that match their own reading ability.

Look out for the Band colour on the book in our Start Reading logo.

The Bands are:

Pink Band 1A & 1B

Red Band 2

Yellow Band 3

Blue Band 4

Green Band 5

Orange Band 6

Turquoise Band 7

Purple Band 8

Gold Band 9

START READING books can be read independently or shared with an adult. They promote the enjoyment of reading through satisfying stories supported by fun illustrations.

Peter Bently lives in Devon with his wife, Lucy and a ready-made audience of two children, Theo (9) and Tara (6). Apart from writing, he enjoys walking, going to the beach, meeting up with friends, and having family fun.

Elisabetta Ferrero works in Vercelli, a town in North Italy surrounded by paddy fields. She lives with her husband and two sons, a hunting dog who loves chasing rabbits but never catches them, six Burmese cats and a gold fish who is 11 years old!